The Naughty-List Elves Save Christmas

By

Nicoline Evans

Author: Nicoline Evans –www.nicolineevans.com

Editor: Emily Kline – www.ekediting.com

Artwork: Allison Rich – www.allisonrichart.com

A special thank you to my beta readers and to everyone who has offered me support during the creation of this book.

Dedicated to those who feel misunderstood

Chapter 1

A snowball hit Sharla Shambles in the face.

"Ow!" she hollered, followed by an immediate laugh. She lowered the large candy jar she was holding and straightened her long, strawberry-blonde braids. She knelt to pack a snowball of her own, and then lifted her gaze with a furrowed brow. "Who dares to challenge me?"

She scanned the village.

No one was in sight.

"Show yourself, scoundrel!"

At her request, five of her fellow naughty-list elves—often referred to simply as naughties— emerged from their hiding places. An onslaught of snowballs catapulted in Sharla's direction.

She screamed, then giggled, as she looked for a place to hide, but there was none.

Jinx Jankie, Ivy Hornswoggle, Figg Filibuster, Coco Corsair, and Rodge Rabblerouser had her surrounded.

"There is no rest for the naughty!" Jinx declared, and his crew of snowball-tossing comrades unloaded on Sharla.

"Why me?" she asked while shielding her head from the ambush.

"You're out here walking alone!" Figg answered as he lobbed a fluffy wad of snow at her. "Easy pickings!"

They threw so many snowballs in her direction that she was waist-deep in a pile of snow by the time they stopped.

"I went to the gingerbreads to refill our community candy jar," Sharla said, pointing at the abandoned jar near the snow pile she was trapped inside. "Next time, I'll be sure to only steal enough candy for myself!"

"Ooh, yum!" Ivy cooed as she abandoned her station to seize the candy-filled jar.

Though Sharla's legs were trapped, her arms were free, and she quickly packed a snowball and lobbed it at Ivy.

"Ouch!" Ivy shouted as the snowball hit her square in the nose.

"Ha! Now, help me out," Sharla demanded.

Ivy wiped the melting snow off her face and began digging Sharla free. Jinx, Figg, Coco, and Rodge hurried to help.

"Did the gingerbreads catch you?" Coco asked, eyes aglow with admiration.

"Would I be here if they had?" Sharla replied with a smirk.

"You're brave," Coco said, still helping the others dig Sharla free. "The last time I tried to refill the candy jar, the gingerbreads spotted me, and as I ran away, they threatened to bake me alongside their next batch of cookies."

"You got caught because you're loud," Figg interjected.

"And slow," Ivy added.

Jinx chuckled. "You couldn't steal from a turtle wearing earmuffs."

"Hmph," Coco grumbled.

"Come with me next time," Sharla offered, almost free from the snow pile. "I'll teach you how to be quick and quiet."

Coco offered Sharla a grateful smile.

"Freedom!" Figg declared as he shoveled the last bit of snow away from Sharla's feet.

"Gee, thanks." Sharla rolled her eyes.

"You got buried so fast," Jinx said, elated by their successful strike. "It was incredible."

"That was a well-organized ambush," Ivy stated, congratulating her and her little team. "Well done!"

They high-fived each other and recapped the prank in furious chatter.

"Couldn't have done it without me," Sharla interjected their revelry. "You're welcome."

Rodge laughed. "Next time, you can be on the winning side."

Ivy gasped, then whispered, "Now's your chance, Sharla. Three goodies approaching—twelve o'clock."

Down the block, three good-list elves turned the corner.

4

"Hide!" Ivy instructed. "And quickly pack some snowballs!"

"Come with me," Figg offered to Sharla.

Sharla lifted her heavy candy jar and waddled to join Figg at his hiding place behind a shoveled snow mound.

She lowered the jar and hurriedly helped him pack snowballs. The recent snowfall allowed for fluffy, soft handheld ammunition.

They had made a pile of thirty when the good-list elves entered the intersection.

Wally Wonder led the trio; Minnie Marvel and Dandy Delight walked beside him.

Jinx held up a fist, alerting his fellow naughties to hold the line.

Figg and Sharla watched Jinx intently, waiting for their cue to strike.

5

Wally, Minnie, and Dandy stopped near the remnants of Sharla's snow pile—it was a strange and out of place messy heap of snow in the middle of the shoveled butterscotch cobblestone pathway.

"This wasn't here this morning," Minnie noted, flipping her sparkling green hair over her shoulder.

"This section of cobblestone was cleared last night," Dandy confirmed.

"Strange," Wally mused. He adjusted his glasses to consult his clipboard of notes.

"Strike!" Jinx shouted as he stood from behind his previously shoveled snow pile and threw the first snowball.

Figg and Sharla stood and did the same, followed by Coco, Rodge, and Ivy.

The good-list elves were under siege.

"Stop!" Dandy shouted.

"My hair!" Minnie shrieked.

"My clipboard!" Wally bellowed.

The naughties laughed and cheered so loudly that they did not hear their objections until the snowy prank ceased. Waist-deep in the remnants of the attack, the good-list elves glared at the naughties with deep contempt.

"Gotcha!" Jinx declared, still proud of himself.

"Of course, you did!" Wally spat in reply. "This was a sneak attack!"

"Well, yeah, that's how pranks work," Jinx explained. "I wish I had a camera! Your faces were priceless."

"Did you get a good laugh?" Wally sneered.

"I did! Didn't you?"

"Does it look like I'm amused?"

Jinx exited his own revelry for the first time to notice the deep lines of anger creasing Wally's typically pleasant expression.

"Oh," Jinx said. "I thought everyone liked snowball fights."

"We didn't like it five years ago, or four years ago, or three, or two, or one! Definitely not now, either. You do this every year, and we never find it funny!"

Jinx lifted his hand to his chin and his face scrunched as he tried to remember.

"I guess it was so long ago that I forgot," he replied, his answer surprisingly genuine.

"So, you're naughty *and* forgetful?" Wally spat. "What *are* you good for?"

"That's mean," Sharla interjected.

"It's the truth!" Wally spat back. "If you can't learn from past mistakes, you'll keep repeating them. Now help us out!"

The naughties shuffled to the center of the cobblestone pathway where the good-list elves were trapped in a large snow pile. As they shoveled their well-mannered counterparts free, Wally continued his lecture. "You know, silly shenanigans are only fun when both parties are equally participating. If it's one-sided, it's no longer fun."

"You don't enjoy *any* shenanigans," Ivy griped as she shoveled.

"That's not true," Wally countered. "Just the other day, we had a wrapping paper tournament at the Good-List Factory. There was a pile of improperly wrapped gifts that needed rewrapping, so we challenged our best wrapping elves to see how fast they could unwrap, toss the ripped paper and bows, and rewrap the gifts."

"It was exhilarating!" Minnie shared.

"Truly thrilling," Dandy agreed.

"It does sound kind of fun," Jinx confessed.

"Why don't you ever play games with us?" Figg asked.

"Because you're always pulling pranks like this!" Wally said, motioning to the remnants of the snowball assault. He held up his wet clipboard. Black ink ran down the page.

"You turn sweet things sour," Minnie added.

"Good times turned bad," Dandy agreed as she readjusted the headband of yellow flowers atop her head.

Ivy huffed, then mumbled under her breath, "Sounds like you're describing yourselves."

The naughties finished shoveling the goodies free.

"Ya know," Jinx explained, "we spend a lot of our time in the dark and dangerous coal mines. We just like to have fun and be silly when we aren't there."

"We have very different ideas of fun," Wally quipped as he brushed any lingering snow off his clothes. "Goodbye!"

Wally marched away, Minnie and Dandy following close behind.

"What did we do wrong?" Coco asked.

"Nothing," Jinx replied. "We just tried to have fun with the wrong people."

He stomped away, agitated.

"Well, that was a rotten time," Rodge noted.

"And they claim that *we* turn everything sour," Ivy added.

No skipping or cartwheeling—Rodge, Ivy, Coco, and Figg followed Jinx back to the Naughty-List Factory. They had a long twenty-four-hour shift starting in the morning.

Sharla lagged behind.

She retrieved the heavy candy-filled jar and wondered, for the first time, if being nice was better than being naughty.

Chapter 2

Deep beyond the snow-covered hills of the North Pole sat the mining tunnels. There, the naughty-list elves slaved away mining chalky black coal for naughty children all over the world. It was thankless work, but they did their job without complaint. Dressed in their uniform mining outfits—beige overalls and hard hats with headlamps—and armed with their pickaxes, shovels, chisels, and buckets, they were ready for twenty-four hours of grueling work.

The naughties trekked out of Christmas Village, through Harmony Forest, and across the Starlight Tundra. To keep their spirits lifted, they sang their work hymn as they walked.

"Heigh-ho! Heigh-ho!
Laughing through the pain, we go!
With jokes and tricks,
shenanigans and mischief.
A little bit bad.
A lotta bit funny.
A little bit mad.
A lotta bit naughty.
A smirk with a wink as we sneak in a trick.
Heigh-ho! Heigh-ho!
Playing pranks as we go!"

Past the Humbug Magic Factory, over the Frosty Hills, and up to Chimney Rock Mines, the naughties stopped singing when they reached the coal mines.

There were five tunnel entrances, two of which were closed for repairs.

Jinx paused, stopping the procession of naughties behind him. He closed his eyes, extended open palms toward the entrances, and felt the vibration radiating from the tunnels.

After a long moment of grave consideration, Jinx lowered his hands, opened his eyes, and led the group into tunnel C.

Wooden beams supported the narrow tunnel every five feet. Some were sturdy, others creaked. Jinx took notes as they walked, jotting down the areas that needed repairs.

Sharla flinched every time she heard the wood crack and splinter. It wasn't too long ago that the naughties had a close call with disaster in tunnel D— one of the beams had snapped in half, causing a tunnel collapse. Luckily, no one had been hurt, but it had taken an entire week to dig the trapped naughties free and a full year to repair that particular mine shaft. They still hadn't returned to tunnel D, and Sharla shuddered as she recalled the danger they narrowly escaped that day.

Two miles into tunnel C, past all their old work stations that were now too fragile to mine, they reached their newest work post.

Each naughty-list elf tied a maroon or teal handkerchief around the bottom half of their face before lifting their pickax and swinging.

Jinx walked behind the line of hammering elves, monitoring their progress and safety. Though the naughty-list elves were often reckless, silly, and mischievous outside of the mines, they never played around inside the mines. They took their job seriously—it was too dangerous not to. Inside the mines, the naughties were focused, organized, and careful.

Jinx paused behind Sharla, who was doubled over and breathing heavily.

"Are you okay?" he asked her.

"My shoulder hurts," she answered.

"Grab your chisel and take a break from the wall. Rodge knocked a huge piece loose. You can rest your shoulder while cracking the fresh lump into tinier pieces."

Sharla nodded and walked down the long line of naughties until she reached Rodge's spot at the far end.

"It's a beaut!" he declared as she knelt beside the giant lump of coal.

Rodge swung his pickax overhead and lowered it into the wall with force. A few more swings would break free another large piece.

Sharla placed her hands on the boulder of coal she was about to chisel.

Chalky black dust covered it.

She spit into her hand and furiously rubbed a spot clean. It took a little work, but the coal sparkled beneath its dusty dirt coating.

Sharla smiled.

Nothing in life was one-dimensional—everything had layers.

"Stop that!" Rodge argued as he caught her cleaning another spot. "It can't sparkle or be pretty. It's for the naughty kids, remember?"

"Maybe those naughty kids are good on the inside and just have trouble showing it. Just like this piece of coal."

"Well then, they need to learn to be good on the outside, too."

Rodge returned to mining the wall.

Sharla did not press the issue. Instead, she removed the chisel and mallet from her toolbelt and chipped the large lump into smaller lumps.

Rodge was right—their job wasn't to reward the naughty children with something pretty. It was to teach them a lesson about being nice. Still, Sharla wondered how many children on that list were just misunderstood.

Unfortunately, Santa only had two lists: the good list and the naughty list.

There was no "misunderstood" list or a "feeling sad or mad, and it comes out as bad" list.

Just bad and good.

Naughty and nice.

The good-list elves built beautiful toys for the good children.

The naughty-list elves mined dirty coal for the naughty children.

Split into two groups, Santa's elves were as different as their jobs.

Orderly, calm, and well-behaved.

Messy, rowdy, and mischievous.

The stark contrast between them was as glaring as the sun when they left the mines after a twenty-four-hour shift.

"Five hours left to go!" Jinx announced.

"Oh, ho ho! I'm ready to throw some snowballs!" Figg Filibuster shouted as he swung his ax.

"Ooh, let's throw some at the nutcrackers!" Ivy Hornswoggle suggested.

The naughties struggled to tame their wildness for a whole day in the mines, and they were beginning to crack.

"While you nerds are tossing snowballs at the blockheads, I'll be sprinkling glitter on the roof of Santa's Workshop," Buzz Buccaneer said with an impish smirk.

"Ha!" Riff Rascal laughed. "He'll think it's angel droppings!"

"Exactly," Buzz confirmed.

All the naughties burst into a fit of giggles.

"Enough!" Jinx shouted, interrupting their revelry. "There is a time and a place for games, and it isn't here. Stay focused!"

"Or," Sharla offered once the giggling subsided, "we could leave everyone else alone for a change."

There was a brief moment of intense silence before her fellow naughties objected all at once.

"That sounds awful!"

"Wretched idea."

"The opposite of fun!"

Sharla took a deep breath to collect her courage. "Maybe there are other ways to have fun."

"If by 'have fun' you mean 'be lame,' then sure," Buzz replied. "We can sit on our hands between mining shifts and just watch the world pass us by."

"Watch where you sit, though," Bonnie Bandit warned with a grin. "It's sap season."

Sharla rolled her eyes and dropped her fight. They'd never listen.

The remaining five hours passed quickly, and as they lined up to leave, Gulliver Knave and Jester Lampoon scurried through the crowd to stand near Sharla.

"We liked your idea," Gulliver offered.

"Yeah," Jester agreed. "Sometimes playing tricks gets tiring. A break sounds nice."

Sharla smiled.

Maybe she wasn't alone in how she was feeling.

Maybe there was some nice hidden within the naughty.

Chapter 3

Back at the Naughty-List Factory, the naughties left a trail of dusty boot prints across the factory floor on their way to the hampers.

No one was bothered by the mess.

They stripped out of their dirty mining clothes and changed into tattered long johns.

Sharla tossed her overalls into the bin with all the other dirty clothes and found an empty upper bunk bed to sleep on.

The following morning, the sound of chaos served as an alarm clock. Her fellow naughties were already awake, dressed, and playing games.

Sharla changed into her favorite maroon tunic and dark green leggings and prepared to face the day.

The other naughties had also changed into their regular outfits—hooded tunics with leggings, long sashes wrapped around flowy blouses, leather strappings and holsters, buttoned vests over ruffled collared shirts.

Ivy and Coco stood near the long row of communal sinks braiding the hair of their fellow naughties. While they twisted and knotted each head of hair into warrior braids, the naughties who weren't in line to get braided ran amuck.

Ruffians armed with candy armor, the naughties played a game of manhunt. Glasses shattered, tables and stools were overturned—nothing stayed nice or neat in the Naughty-List Factory.

Sharla wanted to join. She also wanted to release her stress after working in the mines, but she found herself unable to let go of the heaviness she suddenly carried.

She no longer liked the mess.

She no longer enjoyed the chaos.

Sharla went to the window and stared into the distance—a tiny escape from the madness of the factory.

Shining brightly above the cracked silver bell atop Santa's Workshop, the healing light from the North Star soothed Sharla's unease.

"Come play with us!" Coco Corsair called out to Sharla as she dodged an onslaught of slingshot candies.

Sharla glanced over her shoulder at the mayhem.

Everyone was having fun.

Everyone was happily participating.

The room was filled with laughter and joy.

So, why did everything suddenly feel wrong?

"I need some space," Sharla answered Coco. "I'll play tomorrow."

Coco shrugged and rejoined the game.

The sounds of unruly tomfoolery surrounded Sharla's quiet contemplation.

Then, the boom of a loud explosion brought all the rowdiness to a stop.

"What was that?" Ivy Hornswoggle asked.

Outside the window, in the distance, a large plume of black smoke billowed above the Good-List Factory.

"The Good-List Factory is on fire!" Sharla announced.

"Guess they're not so perfect after all," Ivy scoffed.

"We should go help," Sharla suggested.

"They wouldn't help us," Ivy challenged.

There was a grumbling of agreement among the other naughties.

"It's the right thing to do," Sharla urged.

"She's right," Jinx said, though he looked just as conflicted as the others. "The goodies aren't very nice to us, but if we were in dire need, I think they'd put their dislike aside to help us."

"You really think so?" Ivy asked.

Jinx hesitated. "I certainly hope so."

"I'm going," Sharla declared. She marched out of the Naughty-List Factory, unconcerned whether anyone else joined.

Halfway there, she looked over her shoulder to see a large group of naughties a block behind.

Sharla smiled, happy that they'd get this chance to show the goodies that they weren't just a bunch of troublemaking goofs, but also good, kind, and helpful.

20

The scene at the Good-List Factory was chaotic—the naughties felt right at home.

Good-list elves raced in and out of the building, retrieving as many untarnished gifts as they could. A plume of glittering smoke filtered out the front door.

"What happened here?" Sharla asked Dandy Delight, who was outside organizing all the saved presents.

"The cogs on the gift-wrapping machine got snagged on an improperly tied ribbon, causing the entire contraption to combust."

Sparkling smoke still billowed out of the windows and doors.

"We can help you put out the fire," Sharla offered.

"The fire is already smothered. There's just a lot of lingering smoke."

"Okay, well, let us help you clean up the mess."

"Erm," Dandy mumbled, her eyes darting around for help. "Maybe. Let me see what there is to do."

Wally approached, covered in glittery ash. He dropped an armful of presents near Dandy's feet.

"Why are they here?" he asked.

"They offered to help!" Dandy's eyes held genuine appreciation, but her expression revealed her skepticism.

"No," Wally replied.

"We should give them a chance," Dandy urged. "We really need the help."

"No," Wally firmly repeated.

Sharla stepped forward and demanded, "Why not?"

"You'll just make everything worse," Wally answered.

"No, we won't!"

"Yes, you will. You always do."

Wally marched away.

"He's just in a bad mood," Dandy offered, her tone apologetic.

"Seems he's always in a bad mood around us," Sharla noted.

Minnie Marvel tiptoed with arms full toward the present pile. She added four more charred gifts to the collection.

"Why are they here?" Minnie asked Dandy.

Dandy let out an exasperated huff and returned to her work without answering.

Minnie turned to Sharla.

"Why are you here?"

"We wanted to help, but Wally said no."

"Oh, right. He's in a very bad mood right now." She extended an arm toward the smoking Good-List Factory. "Understandably."

"Why do you all assume the worst of us?" Sharla asked.

Minnie tilted her head and furrowed her brow.

"I thought you liked being the worst?"

"No! We like to have fun!"

"Tricks and jokes and mischief aren't fun for the rest of us."

"Hmph." Sharla crossed her arms over her chest. "We never hurt anyone."

"True, but the aftermath of your tomfoolery often leaves a mess, which makes our job much harder. It's the opposite of fun for everyone but you."

"We can be helpful, too. We know when to be serious and when to be silly—there's a time and place for everything."

"I've yet to see that. Sorry." Minnie gave Sharla a half smile before leaving to join Wally and the other good-list elves in a huddle on the other side of the smoke plume.

Sharla turned to address her fellow naughties and found them wearing looks of insult, outrage, and defiance.

She sighed.

This rejection would not help her bridge the gap between naughty and nice.

Chapter 4

"I knew they'd reject us," Ivy seethed.

"Offering to help was still the right thing to do," Sharla rebutted.

The crowd of naughties trekked back to the Naughty-List Factory in small groups.

Coco Corsair, Jester Lampoon, Gulliver Knave, and Reva Ruffian joined Sharla. When they reached the factory, Sharla hesitated at the door.

"What's wrong?" Jester asked.

"I'd like to keep walking."

"We'll stay with you."

The quintet carried onward, walking past the factory and toward the center of the village.

"They won't even let us try to be good," Sharla said, confiding her worries with her friends.

"I think they like that we're bad because it makes them look extra good," Jester said.

"They aren't good," Reva countered. "They just never have any fun."

"I don't think they know how to have fun," Gulliver agreed.

"Maybe their style of fun just looks different than ours," Sharla rationalized. "Doesn't make either wrong or right, just different. What bothers me most is being labeled as something I am not. I am not always bad; I am not always a troublemaker. And they deny me the opportunity to prove myself otherwise."

"That's just how it is," Jester said with a shrug.

"Well, it's wrong."

As they turned the corner, Santa's Workshop came into view.

Santa stood on the roof wearing an aluminum vest and tinfoil hat. The large headphones covering his ears had a wire that connected his audio to the large metal pole he waved overhead. Santa paced the roof, looking for a signal that likely wasn't there.

"Oh boy," Jester said. "He's at it again."

"Is that his alien or angel communication gear?" Coco asked.

"Aliens. His angel gear is a white satin nightgown."

Sharla grumbled. "Imagine if the worst was assumed about Santa. Imagine if he was judged by his strange activities during his time off instead of the joy he delivers to the world on December twenty-fifth. Christmas would be ruined!"

"Yeah," Jester noted with a grimace. "No one would view Santa the same."

"The jolly man they all know and love is a real oddball when he isn't on the job," Gulliver agreed.

"Who cares?" Sharla countered. "As long as we are taking care of our responsibilities and never causing harm, we should be free to be whoever we please! What's wrong with being quirky," Sharla asked, motioning toward Santa, then placing her hand over her own heart, "or playful? Why can't we find humor in a bit of harmless shenanigans? Why can't we be both silly and serious?"

"I don't know," Reva replied. "Ask all the other Christmas creatures. They're the ones with the issue. We're on your side."

"I want to prove them all wrong."

"How will you do that?" Gulliver asked.

Before Sharla could scheme a plan, tremors shook the village. Loud ground-shaking thuds came from the west.

The naughties turned their attention.

Just above the tree line of Harmony Forest appeared the yule gobbler's head and arms.

The giant sugar monster was heading toward Christmas Village.

Chapter 5

The yule gobbler—a sugar fiend subclass of the abominable snowman species—had almost reached Christmas Village.

This particular yule gobbler stood one hundred feet tall and had irritated eyes dripping with gooey tears of desperation. The red streaks diagonally striped across his white fur were matted with knots and covered his thick sugar skin. He opened his mouth to snarl, revealing his dagger-sharp fangs.

"The end is here!" Santa shouted from the rooftop of his workshop.

Mass hysteria ensued below.

Fleets of nutcrackers shuffled from their military base to the workshop to protect Santa. They transformed the gate into a slanted stake wall.

The Gingerbread Gang emerged from their bakery armed with licorice whips, sugar spikes, four crystallized maple cannons, and scorching hot eggbeaters and whisks. They sauntered menacingly to the edge of the forest, ready to fight if needed.

Sharla and her fellow naughty-list elves stared up at the monster in stunned terror.

"What do we do?" Reva asked.

"If he reaches the village, he will demolish everything!" Gulliver added.

Santa slid down his chimney and reemerged a moment later on his third-floor balcony. He held a megaphone to his mouth, and his voice echoed across the village.

"My lost child," he shouted to the yule gobbler. "Release your anger and discover peace!"

The monster roared.

Violent ground tremors followed.

"I don't think it worked," Sharla noted sarcastically

"Use Christmas magic!" Jester shouted at Santa.

Sharla, Reva, Gulliver, and Coco repeated the request until they caught Santa's attention.

"Magic," Santa whispered, still holding down the button on his megaphone. The word echoed across the sky.

"Yes, magic!" Reva confirmed.

"Sleepiness, blindness, paralysis, a blast of confusion—anything!" Jester encouraged.

Santa retrieved a wooden music box, opened the lid, and revealed a tiny Christmas tree on a spring. He turned the crank, and a quirky melody played. The tree lit up and spun in a slow circle.

He pulled a small wand out of the bottom of the box. It was made out of yule log, wrapped in dried poinsettia petals, and coated in hardened sap. To the music, he chanted a spell no one had heard before, accompanied by an odd dance.

"Oogey woogey boogey boo,
take your anger somewhere new!
Clibby clobby clinging clef,
redirect to somewhere else!"

A blast of glittering dust traveled in a whirlwind and smacked the yule gobbler in the face.

The monster went cross-eyed for a moment, then sneezed and itched his nose. Once the last of the glitter was out of his nostrils, he released a ferocious roar.

"Dang it!" Santa shouted, shaking the stick he had crafted centuries ago. "I think my wand is broken."

"You're not a wizard. You're Santa!" Sharla shouted to him. "You don't need a wand!"

Santa turned his attention to the naughty-list elves standing on the butterscotch cobblestone three floors below.

"I'm not?" he asked. "Hmph. Seems I'm still a bit confuddled. I don't think I've gotten enough rest yet."

The naughties groaned in unison—Santa needed at least three hundred and forty days of rest after Christmas. Come December first, Santa would be his best self again—coherent and jolly ... but it was only October.

"I don't think he'll be the one to save us," Gulliver noted.

The naughties returned their attention to the yule gobbler. Small and unarmed, there was nothing they could do to stop the monster.

The candy cane monster pushed forward, easily knocking down trees in Harmony Forest to clear a path.

He was halfway to Christmas Village.

As Sharla and her friends stood paralyzed in terrified awe, a different group of naughties darted past. They carried slingshots, boomerangs, saltwater guns, bows with sticky-tipped arrows, and rubber ball catapults.

"Join us!" Jinx shouted as they ran by.

"None of that will stop the yule gobbler," Sharla cautioned.

"It's worth a try!"

Jinx and the other naughties ran out of sight.

"We should join them," Jester suggested.

Everyone but Sharla nodded in agreement.

Jester, Reva, Gulliver, and Coco darted off.

Sharla stayed where she was.

Santa was right.

Without a miracle, this would be the end of everything. Christmas would not survive this devastation.

A whirring buzz joined the sound of toppling trees.

Sharla climbed to the roof of the closest gingerbread hut to get a better view.

In the distance, just in the nick of time, the humbugs had arrived. The grumpy, ancient ice creatures flew to the scene of destruction, their icicle wings gleaming in the early evening starlight.

Lassos and harpoons soared through the air, wrapping around the yule gobbler and seizing him where he stood. A sturdy yank by the large fleet of humbugs tugged the monster backward and out of sight.

Though the gobbler was no longer visible, he could still be heard, and he released a final desperate roar.

"GRRAACAAAANNNDDYYYCAAAAANE."

"Did he just say candy cane?" Sharla wondered aloud to herself.

With the yule gobbler knocked to the ground, all that could be seen was the toppling of ancient evergreens as the humbugs dragged him away.

Cheers from every Christmas creature filled the village.

Santa danced alone on his balcony in his long johns.

Sharla found herself wondering how permanent of a solution this was. Would the yule gobbler come back? Would he succeed next time? More importantly, was there a way to stop him before he tried again?

Sharla climbed off the roof and raced to the western side of the village where the gingerbreads, goodies, and her fellow naughties had congregated to fight.

When she got there, their weapons were lowered and they were assessing the damage.

The devastation the yule gobbler had caused to the main trail was visible from afar.

"We can't fix it," Wally said. "We still have smoke billowing out of the Good-List Factory. And we're behind on making presents!"

"Neither can we," Molasses Drizzle, leader of the Gingerbread Gang, said. "We left cakes in the oven. If we don't get back soon, there will be a new fire to squelch."

Everyone looked at Jinx.

He furrowed his brow.

"Don't look at me," he said. "We head back to the mines soon, and decorating is *not* on our list of responsibilities."

"Neither is horsing around or playing pranks," Wally countered.

"We are allowed to spend our downtime however we want."

"Maybe you should spend it helping the greater good of Christmas Village."

"That trail is hardly ever used."

"It is one of four entrances to Christmas Village. Maintaining it is a serious matter."

"That's not a serious job!" Jinx argued.

"We will help!" Sharla interjected from the back of the crowd. "We will do it."

The naughties glared at her in disbelief.

"Hmph," Wally huffed, surprised but accepting. "Excellent. It's settled."

The good-list elves and gingerbreads dispersed, leaving only the naughties at the edge of the forest.

"Why did you do that?" Jinx demanded.

"I have my reasons, and I only need a small team of naughties to help me."

"No," Jinx replied with a huff. "We are in this together."

Sharla smiled, grateful for his solidarity.

The forest cleanup would be difficult, but her ultimate mission would be even harder: taming the yule gobbler.

Sharla looked up at where the monster once stood, tall and fearsome, but also desperate and scared. She could help him. There was good within the bad—she was sure of it.

Chapter 6

"I think we can help him," Sharla announced to a group of naughties back at the Naughty-List Factory.

"Who?" Jinx asked.

"The yule gobbler."

"*Help* him?"

"Yes."

"Yule gobblers have sugar brains," Jinx argued. "They can't see reason or think logically. They are a lost cause."

"They used to be a Christmas creature, just like us," Sharla countered. "Surely they are still in there somewhere."

"I've never seen a yule gobbler revert back to who they were before."

"Maybe they just need help. Maybe they need a guide. Has anyone ever tried to help a yule gobbler?"

"Not that I know of."

"Exactly." Sharla stood tall with confidence. "I'm going to try."

Jinx shrugged. "Don't get squashed in the process."

Sharla looked at the others who were listening to their conversation. "Will anyone help me?"

They stared back at her blankly.

"I will do it alone if I have to," she continued, "but it would be nice to have friends by my side."

"It's a suicide mission," Ivy spoke up. "I'm out."

The majority of nearby naughties followed Ivy into the factory.

"She not wrong, you know," Jester said. "I want to help, but I also don't want to die."

"Do you have a plan?" Gulliver asked.

Sharla hesitated. "I was hoping whoever helped me might help me think of a plan."

Another group of naughties walked away.

Only Jester, Gulliver, Reva, and Coco remained.

"I really think we could help him," she urged.

"Why do you think that?" Coco asked.

"I think he's trying to tell us something, or ask for something."

"All he does is growl and roar!"

"I think there are words hidden in his growls."

Her friends looked skeptical.

"I'll help you," Jester finally offered, "but only if we can get the humbugs to join. They have the weapons and the skills to fight these monsters. If I'm going into the monster's den, I want to have professional monster fighters on my side."

"That's fair," Sharla agreed. She would prefer to have humbug protection, too. "Will you go with me to the Humbug Magic Factory to see if they'll help us? We can clean up Harmony Forest along the way."

Her friends agreed, and after packing overnight knapsacks with tents and tools to fix the forest, they left Christmas Village.

The entrance to Harmony Forest had minimal damage, but a few paces past the tree line revealed the devastation.

Giant evergreens were cracked in half and toppled. Splintered wood and broken ornaments covered the snowy trail.

"It will take years to regrow these trees," Jester griped.

"We'd be better off making a brand new trail," Coco added.

"You might be right," Sharla agreed. "And we can't plant seeds until the spring."

"Looks like we're off the hook to fix the trail," Jester said, faking disappointment.

"We can still clean up the mess."

Sharla tossed shredded tinsel, ornament fragments, and busted twinkle lights into the empty bag she brought.

Her friends followed her lead.

By the time they reached the opposite side of Harmony Forest their bags were full.

Sharla knelt and tied her bag to a nearby tree.

"We'll get them on the way back," she said. "They're too heavy to carry on our long journey."

The small group of naughties left their heavy garbage bags behind and trekked across Starlight Tundra toward the Humbug Magic Factory.

The snowfield was massive and it took a few hours to cross. As the sun set, the North Star shone bright and guided the way.

When they reached the factory, it was evening.

"We're gonna miss our next mining shift," Gulliver warned.

"Jinx knows we're doing a task for the Christmas community," Sharla said, stepping up to the front door. "They'll be fine for one shift without us."

She knocked on the door.

It echoed inside the factory, loud enough to hear from the outside.

A small slit high above the naughties' heads slid open.

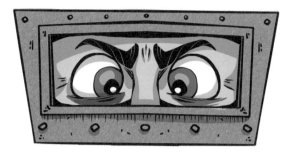

"Who's there?" a grouchy voice asked.

"We're down here!" Sharla said with a wave.

"Who's down there?"

"Sharla Shambles of the naughty-list elves. Plus four of my comrades."

"Naughties?" the voice barked. "Why are you here? I have no record of a scheduled visit." The sound of flipping clipboard pages came through the slit, then he added, "Or an invitation."

"We need your help. Can we speak to the general?"

"Pepper Plump is busy."

"It's important."

The humbug glaring through the slit narrowed his sapphire eyes.

"Empty your pockets," he demanded.

The naughties rolled their eyes and huffed as they obliged.

An assortment of junk fell to the ground: gumballs, candy wrappers, jacks, bouncy balls, marbles, yo-yos, dominos, and playing cards.

Once all their pockets were turned inside out, the humbug guard at the door spoke again.

"You can come inside, but your knapsacks stay outside. And if you do anything naughty, I'll kick you right back out."

"Understood," Sharla said on behalf of herself and her friends.

Jester, Gulliver, Reva, and Coco grumbled in agreement.

The giant door opened and light poured onto the naughties. The humbugs were in the middle of a starlight harvest and the giant contraption in the middle of the factory floor was aglow.

Despite their urge to dance in the starlight, the naughties behaved themselves—the ritual of creating Christmas magic was sacred to the humbugs.

The humbugs sang and the light in their bowls swirled with color.

> *"Mixum, mixum for the yule.*
> *Jumble what we give to you.*
> *Muddled merry, flurries fused,*
> *Starlight cloaked in northern dew.*
> *Zigzag with a crisscross,*
> *mix this into Christmas."*

They repeated the melodic enchantment three times. At the end of their last repetition, the starlight glowed with glittering red, green, gold, and silver.

A new batch of vibrant Christmas magic was created.

The grave and serious energy lifted as the humbugs shuffled around to make paste and liquid out of the newly crafted magic.

Pepper noticed the naughty visitors.

"Rudy! Brutus!" Pepper shouted. "What's the meaning of this?"

"They said it was important," Rudy replied.

"We kept them in line during the ritual," Brutus added.

Pepper eyed his guards before scanning the naughties.

"To what do I owe this displeasure?" Pepper asked.

Sharla ignored the insult. "We came to ask for your help."

"Our help? With what?"

"The yule gobbler."

"Huh? *We're* in charge of the yule gobblers. You just need to stay far, far away from them."

"I think we might be able to help him and prevent a catastrophe, like the one we just endured, from ever happening again."

Pepper shook his head. "We have the monster under control. He won't get that close to Christmas Village again."

"But what if he does?" Sharla pressed.

Pepper's blue eyebrows furrowed. "Are you implying that we are not doing our jobs properly?"

Jester interjected, "I mean, if we're taking recent transgressions into account ... then yeah."

"No!" Sharla objected, side glaring at Jester. "We think we have a way to *help* you with your job."

"We don't need help from mischievous, untrained elves."

Surlie Scrooge, second in command of the humbugs, entered the conversation

"What's going on?" she asked.

"These naughties think they can help us with the yule gobbler," Pepper replied.

Surlie chuckled at the notion.

"Have you forgotten how small you are?" she asked the naughties. "Our ice cannons would break your shoulders."

"We don't want to fight the yule gobbler," Sharla explained. "We want to talk to him."

"*Talk*?" Pepper said. "They don't even speak English!"

"I think they might," Sharla suggested. "I heard the yule gobbler say 'candy cane' within his growl."

"When?"

"When he almost destroyed Christmas Village."

"We were all there," Surlie argued. "None of us heard that."

"None of you were listening."

Surlie huffed.

Pepper crossed his arms over his chest. "Or maybe you're trying to play a prank on us."

"I'm not! I swear," Sharla insisted. "I'm tired of everyone always thinking I'm up to no good. We aren't naughty all the time!"

"There are much easier ways to prove that you have some *nice* in you … and taming a yule gobbler isn't one of them."

"Just hear me out."

"We're listening," Pepper said.

Sharla took a deep breath before speaking.

"All monsters used to be Christmas creatures. They once were just like us!" she explained. "We assume the worst of them, and it's wrong. We ought to listen and try to understand them. Maybe it would save us all from the monster ruining Christmas one day."

Pepper's expression softened. "What do you mean they used to be like us?"

"Don't you know how yule gobblers are created?"

Pepper, Surlie, Rudy, Brutus, and the other humbugs listening shook their heads.

Sharla explained, "They are lost, defeated, or depressed Christmas creatures. They cope with their misfortune by eating tons of sugar. So much sugar, they morph into a yule gobbler."

"How don't you know this?" Jester asked. "You're supposed to be the yule gobbler experts."

"We are experts at fighting them, not understanding them," Surlie replied.

"Well, maybe it's time to understand them a little better," Sharla quipped. "It might make fighting them a whole lot easier."

As they bickered, Pepper was lost in his own thoughts.

"You said they used to be Christmas creatures?" he asked.

"Yes."

Pepper sat with this answer for a moment.

It took Surlie a moment to guess his thoughts, but once she did, her confused expression shifted to shocked disbelief.

"No way! Impossible," she insisted.

"But it *could* be possible," Pepper asserted, unable to shake the hope now coursing through his cold heart.

"What are we talking about?" Sharla asked.

Surlie crossed her arms over her chest and shot Pepper an impatient glare.

Pepper explained, "My father disappeared with a yule gobbler many years ago."

"Crank Christmas!" Gulliver exclaimed. "A true legend."

Pepper mustered a half smile before continuing. "I always assumed that my father was dead—that a yule gobbler killed him—but maybe I was wrong. Maybe he never came back because he got lost and turned into a yule gobbler himself."

"It's possible—" Sharla began.

"No, it's not!" Surlie cut her off. "Crank was the nicest humbug to ever exist. He was also the smartest and most level-headed. He never would have drowned his troubles in sugar. He would have solved them logically."

"But if he was lost deep in the woods, maybe his only options were to adapt or die," Pepper tried to rationalize.

"I know you want to believe that he is still alive, but hope like that is dangerous. If it turns out that it isn't Crank hidden within one of those yule gobblers, you'll be devastated."

"Plus," Rudy added, "humbugs are made of ice. We don't need food or water or anything to survive— just the magic coursing within us. A humbug could survive lost in the woods for an eternity without dying."

"Which means," Surlie further clarified, "if Crank is a yule gobbler, he chose to become one."

"Or his sadness got the best of him," Sharla argued.

"No," Pepper said, finally seeing Surlie's reasoning. "My father was too logical to let sadness win."

"Solitude and sorrow are a dangerous pair," Sharla tried to explain. "It has the power to break the strongest among us."

"I was wrong," Pepper concluded, now angry with himself. "You need to leave."

"Wait! You won't help us? We just want protection. You wouldn't need to do anything else."

"This is a fool's errand," Pepper snapped. "And humbugs are not fools."

Pepper marched away.

"Sorry," Surlie offered.

"You aren't sorry," Sharla snapped, her patience gone. "You convinced him not to help!"

"No, I simply shared my truth. Pepper was only going to help if he believed he was helping his father. And I do not believe that monster is his father."

"It could be another lost humbug!"

"I'm sorry you didn't get what you wanted," Surlie offered again, seemingly genuine.

Sharla growled as she turned and pushed past her fellow naughties.

Sharla was out the door.

"Do you think she'll drop this dangerous quest?" Surlie asked the other naughties.

"Doubtful," Reva answered. "Sharla is stubborn. And she is determined to prove that the naughties aren't always bad."

"Do you agree with her that the naughties have some nice in them?"

"I never thought much about it until Sharla forced the thought upon us." Reva paused. "But I think she might be right. Look at her determination to help a creature less fortunate. I'm starting to think she might be the nicest of all the naughties."

"Maybe nicest of all the Christmas creatures," Gulliver added.

"I think nice is the wrong word," Coco objected. "Anyone can be nice, but not anyone would help a monster. I think the right word to describe Sharla is kind."

Gulliver nodded. "Kindness takes thoughtfulness and effort. That perfectly describes Sharla."

"Regardless," Surlie said. "You ought to get her to drop this quest. You will all get hurt, or killed, if you try to help the yule gobbler without some kind of defense."

"Oh, we aren't going without humbug protection," Jester said. "And hopefully, Sharla will back down when we back out."

Surlie nodded, though her brow remained raised.

As the rest of the naughties left, the question of being good lingered.

Despite all their tricks and tomfoolery, were the naughty-list elves truly more thoughtful than the rest of the Christmas creatures?

Being nice was simple. It was easy—anyone could be nice.

But kindness took effort, consideration, and time. It took great thought and genuine care.

Perhaps the naughty-list elves had been misjudged.

Maybe being kind was superior to being nice.

Chapter 7

Outside the Humbug Magic Factory, Sharla picked up all their discarded pocket items while waiting for her fellow naughties.

When they finally emerged, Sharla handed back their toys, trinkets, and candies with a scowl.

"I don't understand why they won't help," she griped.

"No one has ever tamed a yule gobbler," Reva rationalized. "It's easy to see why the humbugs don't think it's possible."

"Plus, they have dealt with the monsters far more than we have," Gulliver added. "They'd know better than anyone if it's possible."

"Well, I guess we'll have to do it alone." Sharla stood tall and confident.

Her friends fidgeted.

"Erm," Coco muttered. "I don't think that's wise."

"If the humbugs are out, I'm out," Jester declared.

Coco, Reva, and Gulliver nodded in agreement.

"You won't help me anymore?" Sharla asked

"We can't," Coco gently replied. "It's too dangerous."

"You ought to drop this quest, also," Jester advised.

"I won't!"

Sharla swung her overnight bag over her shoulder and marched away, leaving her friends behind.

She hiked across Starlight Tundra, using the well-worn, snow-packed trail that led to Frosty Hills and

Chimney Rock Mines. She knew this route well—she traveled it every few days with the naughties—but she would not go all the way to Frosty Hills this time.

When Merrygloom Forest appeared on her left, she paused.

There was no trail leading into the forest—she would need to make her own.

Sharla took a deep breath and slowly pushed through the deep snow. It was thigh high, turning this leg of her journey into a shoveling exercise.

Using her waterproof gloves, winter boots, and the collapsible shovel she had packed, Sharla pushed, kicked, and shoveled her way toward the forest.

Upon reaching the tree line, the depth of the snow decreased, allowing Sharla to rest for a moment.

The tightly packed evergreen trees, which stood at three hundred to five hundred feet tall, acted as umbrellas and left most of the forest with only a few inches of snow.

Sharla stepped into the dark forest.

The familiar sounds of snow crunching underfoot, arctic birds singing, and the soft patter of fresh snow falling in Starlight Tundra were replaced by dense and deep silence. The only sounds interrupting the eerie quiet were the clicks and clacks of winter bugs and high-above creaks from the trees lurching in the wind.

Five steps into the woods, a low, rumbling cry reached her. Sharla halted, terrified—was the yule gobbler nearby?

The sad growl ceased, leaving only the clicks, clacks, and creaks in the otherwise silent forest.

Many yule gobblers lived in hiding here, but Sharla only hoped to encounter the monster that cried for candy canes. He still spoke their language; his display of intelligence suggested that he might be savable.

Twenty more steps into the forest.

The distant cry did not return.

Another twenty steps.

Sharla was far from her escape route now.

A faraway hum joined the static chittering of the woods. More bugs, Sharla assumed, grateful it was only a hum and not a symphony of howls.

The small trail she followed intersected with a much larger four-way split.

North, south, east, and west—none of which showed signs of where they led.

Before Sharla could make a decision, the sad growl returned, only this time, it was a little more mad than sad.

She shifted her gaze toward the sound and found a pair of glowing red eyes staring at her through the darkness.

"I come as a friend," she blurted.

The angry rumble did not cease.

"I want to help you," she added.

The red eyes lifted out of the shadows as the yule gobbler rose to his feet.

One hundred feet in height, he towered over Sharla, who stood no more than three and a half feet tall.

Shaking violently, Sharla regretted her decision to come alone.

The yule gobbler took a step toward her and released a roar that shook the forest.

"I come in peace!" Sharla shouted, unable to mask her fear.

The monster roared again, ripping a three-hundred-foot tree from its root and tossing it overhead.

Sharla covered her eyes. She did not want to see the end.

During a pause in the monster's furious roaring and destruction, Sharla peeked between her fingers and found the yule gobbler on one knee before her, glaring down at her. His bloodshot eyes held a mixture of desperation and contempt.

He was waiting for her to say something, waiting for her to reveal what she wanted from him.

Sharla lowered her hands from over her eyes.

"My name is Sharla Shambles. I'm a naughty-list elf."

The yule gobbler grunted.

She continued, "Do you have a name?"

His expression tightened as he tried to search for an answer. When the memory did not come, his anger returned. He slammed his giant, hairy fists onto the ground. The force created a tremor that knocked Sharla to her bum.

The yule gobbler's growl turned into a mighty laugh.

Sharla's fear slowly subsided—the yule gobbler wasn't going to kill her after all.

"It's okay if you don't remember. We can pick a new name," she offered.

"Cane," the monster replied.

Sharla smiled as she lifted herself off the ground. "Cane. I like it."

The yule gobbler slammed his fist again, causing another tremor that sent Sharla back to her bum.

His laughter filled Merrygloom Forest.

Though it was at her expense, Sharla couldn't help but laugh, too.

"I bet you used to be a naughty-list elf," she mused.

The sound of the humming bugs grew louder.

Strange, as none of the other sounds in the forest changed volume.

Before she could assess the situation, or make further progress with Cane, the humming turned into a droning buzz, sending her attention upward.

The humbugs.

Sharla scrambled to her feet and waved her arms over her head.

"Everything is okay!" she shouted, but she was too far away, and the yule gobbler's merriment had already morphed back into rage.

"He isn't dangerous!" Sharla tried to explain, but Surlie had already swooped into the forest and seized her by the hood of her jacket.

The other humbugs had the monster lassoed and restrained within a minute of their arrival.

Arms and legs bound, Cane fell onto his side. As he howled a long note of lament, he looked up to Sharla, who was swiftly being carried away.

His sad, angry eyes made contact with her sympathetic gaze.

This time, he released a full roar, forcing every humbug to tighten their earmuffs.

Hidden within the roar, Sharla heard the same word as before.

"Caaaaannnnddddyyyyyyy caaaaaannnnneeeee."

From high above, she smirked, knowing she'd be back to try again.

Chapter 8

"Have you lost your mind?" Surlie shouted down to Sharla, who still hung in her grip.

"He's nice!"

"*Nice*? He almost killed you!"

"We were having fun before you showed up. He only got angry again once you and the other humbugs arrived."

"Tossing trees and causing terrain tremors? You've got a strange definition of fun."

Sharla thought of Cane's fear upon her departure.

"Will he be okay?" she asked.

"He'll be fine. The salt-rope constraints will melt in a few hours and he'll be free to terrorize the North Pole again." The disdain in Surlie's voice was intense. "But if he keeps at it, we might be forced to take more drastic measures."

"Don't hurt him!"

"Right now, I'm only worried about you. You're lucky we followed you."

"Am I?" Sharla snapped.

In response to Sharla's defiance, Surlie swooped lower and, at a safe distance, dropped Sharla into an untouched mound of snow.

"You can walk the rest of the way," Surlie barked. She turned her wings and flew back to her factory.

Sharla grumbled as she climbed out of the snow pile and dusted the flakes off her body.

To her luck, she was already more than halfway back to Christmas Village. Only a short trek across Starlight Tundra separated her from Harmony Forest.

At the tree line, she was pleased to see that her fellow naughties had retrieved their bags of debris. Hers still sat there, so she picked it up and made the trip along the damaged forest trail.

Back in Christmas Village, the Good-List Factory was cleaned up and back in operation. Sharla followed the butterscotch cobblestone until she was home.

The Naughty-List Factory looked as disheveled as ever. Broken twinkle lights lined the chipped and partially melted gutters. Rooftop gumdrops had slid down the icing during a summer heatwave, and no one had climbed up there to repave the icing or reorganize the candy. Sugar chalk graffiti covered the walls, "artwork" designed by the naughties over the years.

Jester stood outside with crumbled cookies in his fist.

Jester smirked. "Yoohoo!" he shouted. "Figg! Buzz! Bolt! Come quick. I need your help!"

As his buddies came running out of the factory, Jester tossed the rest of the cookie crumbles into the sky. The sleet starlings devoured the flying crumbs, then dove for the cookie scraps scattered on the ground.

Jester dodged out of the way, leaving Figg, Buzz, and Bolt caught in the swarm.

Their screams fueled Jester's laughter. His hearty belly laugh echoed for miles.

"That was sneaky!" Figg shouted as he swatted at the birds.

"We'll get you back!" Buzz added.

"I'm sure you will!" Jester said, still roaring with laughter.

The birds finished eating all the crumbs and flew away.

Figg, Buzz, and Bolt were covered in ice-gray feathers and bird droppings.

"This is gross," Bolt said.

"We thought you needed our help," Buzz noted.

"Yeah, we were in the middle of something important," Figg informed Jester.

"What?"

"Coal cutting."

"Well, then get back to it!"

Figg rolled his eyes and stormed back inside.

Bolt shook his head, knocking free some of the feathers, and followed Figg.

"I thought it was funny," Buzz said with a shrug, "and they'll think it's funny later. I'll definitely get you back, though."

"I'd expect nothing less."

Bolt left, leaving Jester alone with Sharla again.

"So, what happened?" he asked. "You're still in one piece."

"The yule gobbler isn't bad!"

"So, you tamed him?"

"No, the humbugs swooped in and evacuated me before I could make real progress. But I learned his name is Cane."

"Wait, why did the humbugs intervene if the monster is good?"

"Well, he was throwing trees and causing ground tremors."

"I thought you said he was being *good*?"

"Wait, how did the humbugs even know I was there?"

"We thought about following you ... then Surlie came out before we left and we told her that you went alone. She got a small crew to follow you, which is why we felt okay leaving."

Sharla grumbled. Grateful that they cared about her safety, but also annoyed because the humbugs had ruined her first attempt.

"I'm going back."

"What's your plan?"

"I'm going to bring candy canes."

"Huh? How will that help?"

"I think that's what he wants."

"But the monster can go to Sugarplum Forest anytime he wants to," Jester argued. "Those are the same candy canes he'd get in Christmas Village."

"You're right," Sharla agreed. "I wonder why he doesn't just get them from there."

"Maybe that's *not* what he wants."

"I'm certain it is. Do you think the gingerbreads would trade candy canes for a deck of playing cards or a slingshot?"

"A slingshot, maybe," Jester answered. "But do they really *need* a slingshot?"

They both shuddered at the thought of giving the gingerbreads more tools to use against them.

"It's worth the risk," Sharla decided. "The yule gobbler is a much bigger problem."

"You might be right."

"Will you join me?"

"Sure, I don't have anywhere else to be."

He was right—they had missed the last shift at the mines and had two days of downtime before returning.

Sharla recruited the same crew as last time: Jester, Coco, Reva, and Gulliver.

The naughties made their way to the enormous gingerbread warehouse on the north side of the village.

Here, the Gingerbread Gang worked as pastry chefs. They were bakers and confectioners—they were in charge of Christmas desserts and candies. And while what they created for the village and the humans beyond was sweet, they were the complete opposite.

The naughty-list elves were the village troublemakers.

The Gingerbread Gang were the village bullies.

This didn't scare the naughties, though. They were the only Christmas creatures brave enough to stand toe to toe with the gingerbreads.

As they approached the warehouse, they tripped an alarm and music blared.

"Ay, Jing-a-di-jing, hee haw hee haw. It's Dominick the Donkey!"

"I hate this song," Gulliver griped.

"I love it!" Coco said, adding a skip and a twirl to her step.

"Now the gingerbreads know we are here," Sharla noted.

As Coco and Jester did cartwheels and jumping heel clicks to the music, Gulliver and Reva trudged forward with their hands over their ears.

Sharla was more worried about the hostile gingerbreads.

As they crossed through the row of tall, stacked gumdrops that bordered the property, ten sticky gum-tipped arrows flew through the sky.

"Take cover!" Sharla warned.

Everyone lifted their knapsacks over their heads except Gulliver, who now had a candy arrow stuck to his forehead.

As he struggled to pull it off, Sharla announced, "We aren't here to cause trouble!"

Another ten arrows flew their way.

Sharla, Reva, Coco, and Jester took cover.

Gulliver was too distracted and got hit in the forehead again.

"Ow!" he moaned, now trying to remove another sticky arrow.

"Give us a chance!" Sharla pled.

A moment of tense silence passed.

"You stole candy from us!" a gingerbread finally replied.

"*Stole* is harsh," Sharla commented. "More like redistributed."

"You aren't welcome here."

"We come with a gift."

"We don't believe you."

"I promise we aren't here to play any tricks."

Another silent moment passed.

"What's the gift?"

"A slingshot."

A few gingerbread heads lifted from behind their chocolate barricades.

"Just one?"

Sharla could now see that Molasses Drizzle led this attack and spoke on behalf of the whole gang.

"What we need isn't worth more than one."

Molasses lowered his nocked arrow, but looked displeased.

Sharla continued, "We gave you those bows and arrows. You know we're good for it."

Molasses marched out from behind his barricade, motioning for the others to stay in armed position.

"What do you want?" he barked at Sharla.

"Candy canes. A dozen in exchange for this slingshot." She held up a beautifully carved slingshot.

66

"I'd accept the trade, except we don't have any candy canes."

"None? How is that possible?"

"The candy cane field in Sugarplum Forest has been barren since September. Luckily, all the other plants and trees are still producing fruit, candy, and sugar. But the peppermint rows are bare."

"Why?"

"Beats me."

"Did you ask the clinkerbells?"

Molasses laughed. "The clinkerbells can't differentiate yesterday from tomorrow."

"They run Sugarplum Forest," Sharla objected. "Surely, they know what's wrong."

"Go ask them yourself, then."

Molasses left, no longer interested in the slingshot.

Sharla turned to her friends.

Jester, Reva, Coco, and Gulliver—who had freed himself of the sticky arrows—awaited Sharla's instruction.

"Looks like we're going to Sugarplum Forest."

Chapter 9

The naughties made their way through the northern streets of Christmas Village until the butterscotch cobblestones grew smaller and eventually faded into the snow.

At the end of the north side of the village sat the entrance to Sugarplum Forest. It was marked by two giant, yellow jelly bean flowers and a purple archway made of braided licorice vines.

The ripe scent of sugar filled the air, and even for the naughties—who loved candy—it smelled a tad too sweet.

"It stinks," Jester protested.

"I feel nauseous," Coco complained.

"Hold it in," Sharla ordered. "We won't be here long."

Sharla and her crew ventured into the forest. She wasn't sure where the clinkerbells would be, but hoped to come across one of them sooner rather than later.

They trekked over the graham cracker bridge that crossed the gushing chocolate river, past the meadow of lollipops, and under a canopy of oozing caramel delights.

No sign of the clinkerbells.

"Where are they?" Reva asked.

"Shh," Sharla replied. "We'll know when we hear them."

The naughties kept their chattering to a minimum and focused on listening.

They walked onward, holding their noses and mouths as the sweet stench grew stronger.

Sweet tart stacks on their right, rock candy quarry on their left—still no sign of the clinkerbells.

When they reached the animal cracker savanna, Sharla paused to admire the majestic creatures.

Cookie-cut elephants, giraffes, lions, tigers, rhinoceroses, and zebras caravanned across the dry landscape with regal grace. To their left was a jungle where the gorillas, monkeys, hippopotamuses, kangaroos, and koala cookies roamed.

"I wonder how long they get to live here before being shoved into one of those little circus boxes for the humans to eat," Sharla said.

"I heard they get to live one hundred years—two full lives—before that happens," Gulliver informed her.

"Who told you that?"

"Santa. I asked him that same question a few decades ago when I first learned about the animal crackers."

Sharla smiled. "I am happy to hear that."

"Same deal for the bears in Gummy Den."

The naughties marched on, now accustomed to the stinky sweetness and no longer holding their noses.

Sugarplum Forest was massive.

They crossed the savanna, walked through a dense thicket of tall cotton candy shrubs and sticky bubblegum webs.

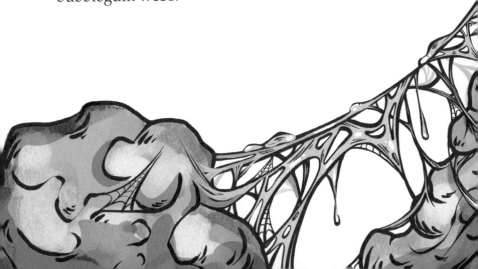

Then, they reached an area Sharla had never seen before.

Before them sat Fireball Volcano. Every few hours, it shot spicy candy balls out of its crater.

"We better reroute," Sharla advised.

As she decided which way to go, the clinking sound of crystallized sugar cracking, breaking, and shattering came from the east.

The clinkerbells were close.

Sharla followed the pretty, chaotic cacophony through a jelly swamp, along a muddy peanut butter trail, and into Marshmallow Valley. Fluffy hills surrounded a field of honey blossoms and pixie stick taffy trees.

Scattered among the field, harvesting honey, powdered sugar, and taffy were the clinkerbells.

Tiny and beautiful, but best known for being fragile and clumsy. Their name came from the tinkling clanks of their bodies breaking and reforming as they moved about.

Their eyes were sparkling diamonds—used to assess millions of sugar granules at once.

Their fingernails were pointed crystals—used to separate and count the minuscule grains with speed.

"Aye!" Sharla shouted from across the field to announce their arrival.

Her shout startled the clinkerbells into a tizzy.

Half of them fluttered in zigzags, slamming into each other as they tried to find a hiding place. The other half shattered into piles of sugar dust, from which they would reform after the naughties left.

Only one stood tall and unmoving.

Unlike the others, who had light touches of color weaved throughout their white and silver outfits, this clinkerbell was all white.

"You must be the leader," Sharla said, embarrassed by the scene of chaos she had accidentally caused.

"I am," the elegant but quirky clinkerbell replied. She wore a sugar icicle crown made of glittery spikes that went across her head from ear to ear. "Leader of the sugar fairies, matriarch of the clinkerbells. My name is Faelynn Featherlace. And yours?"

"Sharla Shambles."

Faelynn took a few steps toward the naughties, her joints shattering with a tinkle. Each step came with corrosion of her crystallized sugar body, but as fast as she broke, she also repaired herself.

"Why have you come to my forest, Sharla Shambles?" Faelynn's outfit was made of tightly wound white feathers and white lace. The style was ancient, intricately woven, and beautiful, but also ragged from centuries of wear and tear. Part farmer, part warrior, it appeared the clinkerbells had a past that they no longer served, but kept alive in their cultural attire.

"I came to speak to you," Sharla answered.

"To me? No one journeys through our diverse terrain to talk to us."

"Well, I did. I think you hold the key to the mystery I'm trying to solve."

"A mystery?" Faelynn's diamond eyes glittered with intrigue. "Do tell."

She lifted to her tippytoes and shuffled closer, raining sparkling sugar dust all around her.

She leaned in close and batted her powder-white eyelashes.

"The candy canes," Sharla revealed.

Faelynn gasped, leaning back and covering her mouth.

"It's a travesty," she said, her voice muffled behind her fingers.

"What happened?"

"Where to begin … " Faelynn tilted her head in consideration. The spikes of her crown shimmered in the sunlight. "I suppose the blame lands on us."

"You ate them all?"

"We don't eat what we grow!" Faelynn exclaimed with a chuckle. "Any more sugar and we'd rot."

"Then you demolished the field?"

"We don't sabotage our crop fields!"

"I'm confused," Sharla confessed.

"Why would we destroy an entire field of candy canes?" Faelynn paused. "Unless, of course, they were contaminated or had an infestation. But the candy cane field was in perfect condition."

"Then how is it your fault?"

"Because the forest is our responsibility!"

Sharla was beginning to understand why the gingerbreads didn't bother asking the clinkerbells for help—they were very kind, but aloof. They wanted to be helpful, but often weren't.

She, too, was losing her patience.

"But what *happened*?" Sharla asked, hoping to get some solid answers.

"Come with me," Faelynn said, waving Sharla and the other naughties forward as she tiptoed in the opposite direction.

She led them past the marshmallow hills, through a nougat marsh, and into a bonbon blockfield.

Chocolate boulders filled with various sweet fillings covered this part of Sugarplum Forest. Faelynn didn't have wings, yet she easily fluttered up, over, and around the giant bonbons, whereas the naughties had to climb, jump, and scramble.

"Where are you taking us?" Sharla asked as she and the other naughties followed.

"To my house!"

"Why, though?"

"We're here!" Faelynn announced.

The naughties paused their clambering and scanned the area in confusion.

There were no structures in sight.

"We are?" Jester asked.

Faelynn giggled, then dove into a small hole at the top of the nearest bonbon.

The naughties jumped and climbed to get to the bonbon she disappeared within.

Once all five were there, they knelt and peered into the opening.

Shabby yet cozy, Faelynn's home was carved into the buttercream ganache that filled this particular bonbon. Intricate and fragile, soft and sticky.

"Come on down!"

"We are too big," Sharla replied.

"Yeah," Reva added. "We would smush everything."

"Do you all live like this?" Gulliver asked.

"No," Faelynn answered. "Some clinkerbells make homes inside old pots, jars, and boxes. They fill their homes with trinkets and charms they've collected. Others live tucked away in sugar tree nooks, hidden in cotton candy alcoves, inside honeycombs, in the caves behind the white chocolate waterfall, or within the recesses of large chocolate boulders."

"Can you please tell us what happened to the candy canes?" Sharla pled, aggravated.

"Oh, right! Now I remember why I brought you here."

Faelynn disappeared into a room the naughties could not see.

"We should've listened to the gingerbreads," Jester grumbled. "This is a waste of time."

Faelynn reemerged holding a bouquet of candy canes.

"For you!" she announced.

She lifted herself off the ground, lightly kicked her feet, and rose to where the naughties still leaned over the bonbon opening.

"Thank you," Sharla expressed, accepting the candy cane bouquet. "But this will only fix the problem temporarily. We need to repair the candy cane field."

"We keep trying, but it's not an easy fix," Faelynn explained. "And every time we get close, we are whisked away to solve a different problem."

"What could be more important than fixing the candy cane field?" Coco asked. "It's the most popular Christmas candy!"

Her answer came in the form of thudding footsteps.

A yule gobbler was in their midst.

Chapter 10

On the other side of the bonbon blockfield approached a giant yule gobbler with chocolate-stained fur. Empty eyes made of chocolate nonpareils covered in tiny white sprinkles, lips made of caramel buttercream, and teeth sharp as daggers, this yule gobbler was a chocolate nightmare.

The naughties threw their bodies over the opening of the bonbon and hung by their arms. Faelynn hovered in the center of the opening. They watched in silent horror as the monster gobbled up fifteen bonbon boulders, burped loudly, and then stumbled away in a sugar stupor.

As soon as it was gone, a manic team of clinkerbells emerged from the forest surrounding the bonbon blockfield and got to work restoring what the yule gobbler had destroyed.

"Wow, the gobblers are gluttonous!" Sharla commented.

"They're just sad," Faelynn replied.

Sharla realized she was falling into the old habit of making assumptions without really knowing.

"You're right," she confessed. "But I'm sorry you have to frantically rebuild what they devour."

"This is why we never have time to fully fix the candy cane field," Faelynn explained. "There's always a gobbler destroying some other part of the forest."

"Do you think a yule gobbler wrecked the candy cane field?" Sharla asked.

"I'm not sure … we've never seen damage like that before. We've never been unable to fix it before, either." Faelynn sighed. "I have to help the others rebuild the bonbons. I'm sorry I wasn't more help."

"Where is the candy cane field?" Sharla asked.

"To the west. Past the white chocolate waterfall." She pointed them in the right direction before departing.

Sharla and her crew were alone again.

"If they can't fix it, how do you suppose we will?" Jester asked Sharla.

"I'm not sure, but we have to try. We have to mollify the candy cane yule gobbler—the survival of Christmas depends on it."

A short walk west through the taffy tree forest led them to the massive white chocolate waterfall. Impressive in both size and flow, the naughties paused to appreciate its beauty.

As they carried onward, they entered a maple grove. The trees were spiked with spiles that dripped sugar sap into tin buckets.

Next up, an apiary where honey was farmed. Countless beehives hung from tree branches, and inside each beehive were decadent, gooey honeycombs. The land was overgrown with beautiful wildflowers that lined the numerous rows of bee boxes where additional honey was made.

Honeybees swarmed the naughties with curiosity as they walked through.

"Don't panic," Sharla advised. "They're just curious. They won't sting you if you stay calm."

"How do you know?" Coco asked between deep, worried breaths.

"After they sting, they die. They can only sting once, and they won't waste it on you if you aren't a threat."

The naughties heeded her warning, stayed calm, and made it through the apiary unscathed.

They reached the candy cane field.

Brittle remnants of the candy canes protruded from the ground in neat rows, but they were gray and no longer sweet. The entire field was covered in sparkling white dust.

The naughties looked on in perplexed awe.

"What do you think it is?"

"Something that counteracts sugar magic," Sharla guessed. She walked into the field, retrieved a pinch of the white granules, and sniffed them. "Smells tart."

"Is it food?"

Sharla carefully touched the tip of her tongue to the sparkling dust. Upon contact, she immediately retreated.

"Blek! It's sour salt!" she announced.

"Sour salt?"

"Tart and tangy!" Sharla thought for a moment. "This is humbug salt!"

"Why would the humbugs ruin this candy cane field?" Coco asked.

"They hate sugar, but I don't think they'd actively seek to destroy this field."

"And if they had, why not destroy the whole forest while they're at it?" Gulliver added.

"Because they didn't do this," Sharla stated. "They would never. Santa needs sugar to fuel his sleigh, and the reindeer need a mix of Christmas magic and sugared carrots to fly. The humbugs are a lot of things—grumpy, grouchy, and cross—but they would never sabotage Christmas."

"Then how did their bitter brand of salt get all the way into Sugarplum Forest?"

Sharla remembered the dusty yule gobbler she met in Merrygloom Forest.

"I think Cane brought it here by accident!"

"Who is Cane?" Jester asked.

"The red and white striped yule gobbler. The one who almost destroyed Christmas Village. The humbugs use salt bombs to subdue the monsters. It must have come here to feast on candy canes after an altercation with the humbugs."

"And salt is the foe of sugar," Reva added. "No wonder the clinkerbells' sugar magic couldn't fix this mess!"

"Yeah, but how do *we* fix it?" Gulliver asked.

"What's the foe of salt?"

"Water," Sharla answered.

"Water will dissolve sugar, too, though," Reva said.

"Yes, but once this field is stripped and the salt is gone, the clinkerbells' magic will work and they can rebuild."

"How will we get enough water here to drench this huge field?" Jester asked.

A twinkle of mischief gleamed in Sharla's eyes.

"Christmas magic," she answered.

"We were forbidden from handling Christmas magic eons ago," Coco griped.

"The good-list elves won't let us near the pipes," Gulliver added.

"Well, we need it to save Christmas," Sharla said. "If we don't satisfy the yule gobbler's appetite for candy canes, he'll keep coming to Christmas Village and demolishing everything in his path along the way."

"Does he think he'll find candy canes in the village?" Coco asked.

"It seems so."

"And how will we acquire Christmas magic for this task?" Jester asked.

"We'll go to the big man and ask for it directly."

"Santa?" Reva asked with one eyebrow raised. "He's usually not too helpful this time of year."

"Yeah," Gulliver added, "his brain lives elsewhere until December first. One time, I think he thought he was a bird."

"Exactly." Sharla wore a sneaky smile. "He'll lend us some Christmas magic without any fuss at all."

The other four naughties lit up with excitement.

"Let's go!"

The naughties backtracked through Sugarplum Forest.

When they reached the bonbon blockfield, Sharla located Faelynn and shouted, "We figured out the problem. It's humbug salt!"

"How did humbug salt get here?"

"On the back of a yule gobbler. We're going to send rain."

"No!" Faelynn shrieked. "Rain will destroy everything!"

"Localized rain, just over the candy cane field. That entire area needs to be completely dissolved before you can rebuild."

"Please be careful!"

"We will," Sharla promised.

The naughties left Sugarplum Forest, excited to use magic to save Christmas.

Though they'd have to be clever and sneaky, and might need to do a bit of "borrowing," they knew their intentions were good. They might be seen as naughty once again, but they were confident it was for the greater good.

Chapter 11

At Santa's Workshop, the nutcrackers standing guard raised their swords at the sight of the naughty-list elves.

"Naughties are not welcome inside!" General Günter Chestnut declared.

"No naughty-list elves allowed!" Major Claramond Hazelnut added.

"We need to speak to Santa," Sharla requested.

"Santa is in no state to be spoken to," Major Hazelnut replied.

"Still, we must."

"Request denied," General Chestnut shouted. His voice echoed for miles.

As the booming ricochet of his voice diminished, a moment of tense silence lingered between the nutcrackers and the naughty-list elves.

Sharla elbowed Gulliver in the ribs, causing him to snap his head toward her in anger, but when he saw the gleam in her eyes, he immediately knew the plan.

Gulliver interrupted the tense quietness with a fit of hiccups.

"What's wrong with him?" Major Hazelnut asked.

"He must have air bubbles trapped in his chest," Sharla answered. "Chocolate-covered nuts always help."

She reached into her pocket and retrieved eight chocolate-covered gumballs.

General Chestnut leaned forward, nostrils flaring, trying to catch the scent of his favorite treat.

As Sharla turned to face Gulliver, she tripped over herself and the eight candies flew into the air and rolled toward the nutcrackers.

The nutcrackers eyeballed the candies, then the naughties, then each other, before stiffly racing each other to seize the candy.

The naughties did not fight to get to the candy first; they simply observed with devious smirks on their faces as each nutcracker popped a chocolate-covered gumball into their mouth.

The taste of chocolate masked the bubblegum flavor at first. They chomped and chomped, and by the time they realized there were no nuts inside, the gum had become so sticky, the nutcrackers could barely open their mouths.

"What is this?" Major Hazelnut demanded in a muffle—the bottom of her wooden mouth was glued to the top. She lifted her hand to rip the gum out of her mouth, but now her hand was stuck, too.

The more they moved and tried to free their mouths, the worse their situation became. Mouths glued shut, hands stuck to their faces, they wobbled and fidgeted in a panic.

Captain Fritz Pistachio toppled into Lieutenant Ludwig Cashew. He caught himself with his free hand, which landed on the lieutenant's face and cemented them together this way.

Sergeant Matilda Walnut stumbled and her head smacked into Corporal Lieselotte Peanut's shoulder, where Lieselotte had recently stuck some of the gum from her mouth. Now, they were trapped together in this awkward position.

"The lot of you are a disaster!" Sharla announced with a laugh.

"It's gum!" General Chestnut mumbled, his fury useless as both of his hands were stuck to his mouth. "You tricked us with gum!"

"It's for the greater good," Sharla promised.

She and the other naughties darted between the nutcrackers' long and lanky wooden legs.

The nutcrackers grumbled and teetered where they stood guard, infuriatingly bound to themselves and each other by bubblegum.

Sharla paused and glanced over her shoulder at the helpless nutcrackers.

"Vinegar should help! I'll see if Santa has any," she offered with a wink before turning back around and running inside the workshop.

Chapter 12

Santa's Workshop wasn't really a workshop at all. It used to be, but when the good-list and naughty-list elves vacated the building decades ago to build their own factories, Santa's Workshop was abandoned.

Now, long rows of dusty tables and benches lined an empty workspace.

The naughties walked through the ghost land of Christmas past, trying not to recall their horrific memories from the Elf War. Back when all elves were the same, when all elves were created equal—they had all lived through it, but no one ever talked about it. It was too traumatizing, too painful.

Ancient machinery sat under giant tarps, likely broken from years of neglect.

Two sets of staircases encircled the deserted workshop. On the second story were Santa's living quarters.

The naughties climbed the steps and paused at the giant doors separating Santa's home from the forsaken workshop. Light filtered through the crack where the two doors met.

"Should we knock?" Coco asked.

"I say we just go in," Jester replied.

"Let's not start off on the wrong foot," Sharla advised before lightly rapping her fist against the door.

A few long moments passed with no response. She tried again.

This time, a little body blocked the light filtering through the doors and a tiny voice shouted through the crack.

"Why are you here?" the shaking voice asked.

"To speak to Santa," Sharla answered.

"He's not taking visitors."

"Who are *you*?" Sharla challenged.

The little voice squeaked, "I am a mulligrub."

"I know *what* you are. I'm asking *who* you are."

"My name is Calum."

"Please let us inside, Calum."

"I was told no visitors."

"By who?"

"Mrs. Claus."

Sharla paused to refocus her approach.

She said, "You know what's fun ... "

"What?"

"Bending the rules a little."

Calum squeaked. "No, no. Mulligrubs never bend the rules."

Jester chimed in, "That's because you're a bunch of scaredy cats."

"Not scared," Sharla said to lessen the insult, "Just cautious.

"Yes! We're just cautious."

"You don't want to mess things up," Sharla added.

"Exactly."

"What if I told you that the survival of Christmas relied on this meeting with Santa?"

"Survival?" Calum asked. "Christmas is in danger?"

"Yes."

"Oh, dear." Calum hesitated. "And you can save it?"

"We can."

Calum let out a deep sigh, then asked, "Do you *promise* not to cause any trouble?"

"Of course. We don't want to create problems for Santa."

The sound of Calum dragging a step ladder screeched for all to hear.

He then unlocked the door, which swung open with Calum still hanging from the doorknob.

He was much smaller than the naughties and goodies.

The mulligrubs were pixie elves— scrawny, tiny, and ruled by their nerves. Unlike the other Christmas elves, mulligrubs did not possess holiday cheer. Instead, their strength came from nature. They lived in Santa's garden—which was situated in a greenhouse in the eastern wing of his home—and they made healing potions and brews out of flowers, herbs, and roots. They were the reason Santa could live forever. They kept him healthy despite his ancient age.

Mulligrubs' bodies were made of woven blades of grass, leaves, ferns, and pine needles.

Atop their heads, some wore flowers—bluebells, dandelions, orchids, dahlias. Others sported lush tree branches, ferns, mossy caps, or grass.

Calum had a lion's mane mushroom cap with flowing white tendrils.

Some mulligrubs wore outfits made from flowers—tulip skirts, peony tutus, rose petal trousers, iris blossom blouses. Other mulligrubs wore mossy overalls, pinecone armor, fiddle fern strappings, evergreen sweaters.

Calum wore a thigh-length vest made of orange and yellow autumn leaves.

Each mulligrub specialized in a different type of healing power.

"What's your specialty?" Sharla asked Calum as the naughties helped him down from the doorknob.

"Brain health—memory, focus, mood, cognitive function, and sensory."

"I think you need to increase the dosage of whatever you're giving Santa," Jester said. "His neurons are misfiring."

"He's perfectly fine," Calum scoffed.

The naughties shared a look of disbelief, but did not challenge the mulligrub.

"Speaking of Santa," Sharla said. "Where can we find him?"

"In the solarium. It's almost time for his stargazing session." Calum's voice was filled with wonder.

"More like alien hunting," Jester mumbled.

Gulliver and Reva chuckled.

"Can you lead us there?" Sharla asked.

Calum nodded, still trembling, and led the way.

The solarium doors were made of semi-translucent purple epoxy and decorated with yellow stars of varying sizes.

"I'll leave you to it," Calum said before scurrying away.

Sharla knocked.

"Who's there?" Santa barked.

"Your favorite naughty elves," she shouted in reply.

"Come in."

The naughties opened the door and shuffled inside.

Santa wore a scowl while squinting at them.

"Who did you say you were?" he asked again, still sitting in his recliner next to a large telescope.

"You know who we are!" Sharla challenged.

"Hold on a minute." Santa retrieved a pair of glasses wedged beneath the cushion of his seat. Their crystal lenses had giant swirling circles carved into them. Santa put them on—his eyeballs were now magnified and distorted.

He smiled. "Ah, now I can see straight. Charlotte, Reba, Oliver, Chester—" he adjusted his glasses "— and cute little Loco. To what do I owe the pleasure?"

The group of naughties snickered as Santa butchered their names.

Sharla stepped forward.

"We are here to ask for Christmas magic."

"What for?"

"We need it to save Christmas."

"To save Christmas?" Santa barked. He pressed his fingers to the sides of his forehead and massaged his temples. "I just spoke to the aliens yesterday! They swore they came in peace this time."

"This time?" Coco asked.

"Yes, last time they said they'd call the cops if I ever shimmied down their chimney again." Santa paused. "Or was that the humans … "

"We're not saving Christmas from the aliens, or from humans," Sharla interrupted, steering the conversation back on course. "We're saving it from a particularly hopeless yule gobbler. He accidentally ruined the candy cane fields in Sugarplum Forest, and now he keeps trying to invade Christmas Village to steal candy canes from here."

"The gobblers," Santa said, his tone flat but his eyes glimmering with deep sorrow. "My lost friends."

"Yes, we want to help this one by clearing the field of humbug salt so the clinkerbells can regrow the candy canes."

"You want to give the creature more of what's killing him?"

"Candy canes aren't killing him."

"I guess the truth varies based on the lens you're looking through." Santa fussed with the glasses sitting on the bridge of his nose. Lifting and lowering, then lifting again. "No," he finally stated, lowering his glasses. "Sugar is not his friend."

"Perhaps not," Sharla said, her frustration growing, "but it *is* a bandage. And a temporary fix is better than no fix at all."

"Have I ever told you about the time the hitch of my sleigh broke over the Caribbean Sea and a pirate helped me fix it?" Santa asked.

The naughties replied with blank stares.

Santa continued, "Well, after the pirate performed a quick fix, the hitch broke again midair and my sleigh fell into the sea. I had to ride Donner the rest of the night." Santa paused. "I should've known better. Pirates fix ships, not sleighs."

"Santa—"

"And you can't ride a reindeer like you would a horse. Well, you can, but don't expect a smooth ride."

"Santa!" Sharla shouted.

"The point," Santa continued, "is that a quick fix is never better than a proper fix. And sometimes, it can make the problem worse."

"Then let's make a deal."

"Oh, how fun!" Santa clapped his hands.

"We will use this quick fix to get us to Christmas, then we'll visit the yule gobbler during the year to see if there's something more permanent we can do to help."

"It's a solid offer." Santa rubbed his chin. "Do you think the aliens would accept a similar offer? They want my body, but perhaps they'd accept a few hair clippings?"

"Where is Mrs. Claus?" Sharla asked.

"My love!" Santa beamed. "She's baking puffed cream pies with the mulligrubs. Why do you ask?"

"She needs to take your temperature."

"Ho, ho, ho!" Santa laughed, placing his hand on his forehead. "I'm cooler than an ice cube in June."

"That's … not good."

"What were we talking about? The angels—"

"No," Sharla interrupted, "letting us borrow some Christmas magic."

"Why didn't you just say that to begin with!" Santa chuckled and stuck his hand into his recliner chair again. This time, he pulled out a snow globe.

"Do you know how to use it?" he asked.

She shook her head.

Santa stood and tapped his foot. The offbeat rhythm, to him, was a perfect steady tempo.

"Give it a shake," he sang. *"Let the snow swirl."*

Santa shook the snow globe, disturbing the sleeping snowflakes.

"Count to three and prepare your words."

Santa closed his eyes and counted.

"One."

Hip bump to the left.

"Two."

Hip bump to the right.

"Three."

Hip bump to the left.

With a giant smile on his face, Santa opened one eye to see if the naughties were enjoying his performance.

Only Coco was bopping up and down to the unsteady tempo.

He continued, smile still gleaming. *"A wish is a trick! Be careful with your words, or your wish might turn absurd!"*

Toe still tapping, Santa lifted the snow globe closer to his mouth and whispered something the naughties couldn't hear. He loudly ended his whispered wish with the word, *please.*

"Every wish must be polite. If you don't say please, the magic won't ignite."

As Santa finished his song, the wish he expelled took shape. It first came with a rumble, then a loud yelp from Jester.

"Oh, Chester!" Santa said with a chuckle. "You sure are cute."

The naughties turned to face Jester and immediately burst into a fit of laughter.

The tough guy naughty-list elf was now a precious pink bunny with glittering eyelashes and big, gleaming eyes.

Jester tried to protest, but all that came out were tiny, adorable squeaks.

This sent the naughties into a greater giggle fit.

"Ho, ho, ho!" Santa belly laughed. "Alright, now. Charlotte—give the magic snow globe a try. Return Jester to his normal self."

Sharla's cinnamon eyes were aglow as she took the beautiful snow globe from Santa.

She shook it, counted to three, and then whispered, "Return Jester to his normal self, please."

With a puff of smoke and sparks, Jester morphed back into a naughty-list elf.

"Why me?" he asked, touching different parts of his body in a panic to make sure everything was back to normal.

Santa smiled and sang a little jingle as he returned to his telescope.

"I hear you when I'm sleeping. I see you when I wake. I know when you are cruel or mean, so be kind, for goodness sake."

The naughties side-eyed Jester, who now slouched in shame—he had made a lot of nasty comments today, and Santa had heard it all.

The naughties shuffled out of Santa's solarium.

Sharla playfully pushed Jester, who was wallowing in regret.

"Don't beat yourself up. Just do better moving forward," she advised.

Jester gave her a half smile.

Sharla stepped to the front of the group, held the snow globe over her head, and declared, "It's time to save Christmas!"

Chapter 13

"We're going to make it rain over Sugarplum Forest?" Coco asked as they exited Santa's living quarters and reentered the abandoned workshop.

"Just over the candy cane fields," Sharla answered.

"Why don't we just make a batch of candy canes, give it to the yule gobbler, and call it a day?" Gulliver asked.

"Because that's a far quicker fix than the quick fix we're trying to orchestrate," Sharla explained. "Even if we made a dozen canes, he'd eat them all in a day and be ravenous for more. Fixing the field is the right move." Sharla paused in thought. "But I will make a few more candy canes to add to the bouquet Faelynn gave me. That should hold him over while the clinkerbells regrow the fields."

Sharla shook the snow globe, counted to three, then said, "Twelve candy canes, please."

Twelve candy canes tied together by a red ribbon appeared in her grip.

"Incredible," she said in awe.

"Do you think Santa will remember giving the snow globe to us?" Jester asked, his smile curling at the ends. "Maybe we can keep it."

"We could have a lot of fun with magic like that," Reva added, her eyes aglow with trouble.

"Shh!" Coco insisted, then whispered, "He can still hear us!"

"You never learn," Sharla said, shaking her head in disapproval. "Of course, we are giving it back. And if you aren't careful," she said to Jester, "he might turn you into a pink rabbit permanently next time."

They exited the workshop to the chaotic scene they had caused earlier—bubblegum-bound nutcrackers.

"Help!" General Chestnut managed to mumble through the closed blocks of his mouth.

"Oops," Sharla said to herself. She shook the snow globe, counted to three, and said, "Jugs of vinegar for the nutcrackers, please."

Three glass jugs filled with potent vinegar appeared at the nutcrackers' feet.

"I'd help, but I'm afraid you'll try to arrest us once you're untangled," Sharla explained.

The nutcrackers grumbled inaudibly. It was hard to tell if they were angry or desperate, making threats or pleading for help.

The naughties left.

Sharla watched over her shoulder as the nutcrackers hobbled awkwardly, all stuck together, toward the vinegar jugs. It was their only escape from the sticky, gummy confines.

She turned back around and a foreign feeling of guilt seized her heart.

The trick was harmless, mostly.

The nutcrackers would get back to normal, eventually.

Sharla sighed, thinking that she might still have a lot left to learn also.

For now, she needed to focus on her mission.

She led the group of naughties back to Sugarplum Forest. Instead of going straight after the flowery entryway, they turned west.

The long trail was lined with sugar-coated sour gummy blossoms and tall caramel popcorn plants. The trail led them into a colorful candy apple orchard with lush fruit covered in a sweet glaze. When they reached the white chocolate waterfall, they knew they were close.

The naughties trekked through the maple grove and honey apiary quickly.

At the edge of the apiary sat the candy cane field. It was as dead as it had been during their last visit.

"Time to make it rain," Sharla declared, taking the snow globe out of her satchel. She shook it, counted to three, and then whispered, "Send an isolated rainstorm over the candy cane field, please."

At her command, a perfectly concentrated rain shower poured over the dead field. The raindrops only hit the candy canes and nothing else.

As the salt dissolved, so did all the rotten candy.

Around the field, clinkerbells emerged, standing just outside the range of the storm. The tinkling of their shattering joints paired nicely with the pitter-pat of the rain.

Everyone watched as the severely damaged field was stripped and restored.

Once all the salt and sugar dissolved, Sharla shook the snow globe, counted to three, and whispered, "Make the rain stop, please."

The storm vanished and the sun returned.

Faelynn fluttered into the middle of the field and sniffed a handful of the regenerated soil. She then touched her tongue to it.

Sharla shouted from the edge of the field.

"What's the consensus?"

"Smells and tastes fresh," Faelynn replied. "I think we can finally regrow the candy cane field."

"Excellent!"

"Thank you for your help!" Faelynn offered.

"Seems there's a bit of nice hidden beneath all the naughty."

The clinkerbells scurried into the field, their sugar-crystal bodies cracking as they moved and showering the field with fertilizing sugar.

"So ... did we save Christmas?" Coco asked, unsure if their job was done.

"Almost," Sharla answered. "I just need to deliver the candy cane bouquets to the yule gobbler to keep him from ruining the village before the field is regrown."

"You're going to visit him again?" Coco asked with a shudder.

"Don't worry, you don't need to come. I can do that on my own."

The naughties began their journey out of Sugarplum Forest. As they reached the trail of sugar-coated sour gummy blossoms, the distant roars of an irritated monster reached them.

"Oh no," Sharla said before turning her stroll into a frantic run. The naughties dashed to the end of the trail and through the flowered archway.

On top of the hill, they could see over and beyond Christmas Village to Harmony Forest.

Walking down the same path he had previously destroyed was the candy cane yule gobbler. Humbugs swarmed his head, but he swatted them away effortlessly.

"He's back," Reva said with a horrified gasp.

"No," Sharla said before darting toward the monster.

"Stop!" Reva shouted after her. "He's too angry! He'll hurt you!"

But Sharla did not stop.

Not only did she wish to save Christmas, but the yule gobbler, too.

Only she could help him now.

Chapter 14

The humbugs would kill the yule gobbler this time—Surlie had said they would the last time they spoke.

While running, Sharla shook the snow globe, counted to three, then made her wish.

In a blink, her wish was granted, and she was now sitting on the raging yule gobbler's shoulder.

Though she was tiny, he felt her there, and his fury increased. He lifted his arms and spun in circles, flailing around violently.

Sharla clutched to his sticky fur so she wasn't bucked off.

"Whoa, buddy!" she shouted. "I'm here to help!"
A humbug buzzed closer.

"What are you doing?"

Sharla looked up to see Surlie Scrooge shouting down at her.

"Don't kill him!" Sharla pled as the gobbler reared and resisted her assistance.

"He's given us no other choice," Surlie replied. "He's attacking the village again, and we are obligated to protect Santa and Christmas."

"I can tame him. Give me a chance."

"You aren't doing a very good job."

"If you leave, he might calm down. He doesn't like humbugs."

Surlie crossed her arms over her chest and huffed.

"Fine," Surlie conceded. "We will elevate to a higher altitude, but if he takes one step closer to the village, we will return and finish this job."

Sharla shook her hand at the humbug, shooing her away.

Once Surlie and the other humbugs had retreated to a higher elevation and the buzz of their flapping ice wings was no longer audible, the yule gobbler's resistance lessened.

"Hey, Cane," Sharla offered.

Cane whimpered.

"Do you want to go home?" she asked.

"Home," Cane repeated in a growl, looking over his shoulder. He then returned his gaze to Christmas Village and his bloodshot eyes narrowed. "Candy canes."

He released a hungry roar.

"I brought some for you!"

But it was too late.

The yule gobbler's mind had refocused on his original mission and he couldn't hear her. He was transfixed on the ornamental candy canes decorating the many gingerbread cottages in the village.

Cane took a single step toward the village and the menacing buzz of humbugs returned.

Panicked, Sharla shook the snow globe, counted to three, and made another wish.

In a blink, the furious sound of war vanished, and she and the yule gobbler were back in Merrygloom Forest.

Cane scanned his sudden and new surroundings with confusion before releasing a loud roar.

"No candy canes here!" he bellowed.

"Yes, there are. I brought some for you. Help me down."

Cane lifted his hand to his shoulder, which Sharla carefully climbed onto, and he lowered her back to the ground.

She reached into her satchel and retrieved both candy cane bouquets.

Upon seeing them, Cane transformed from a feral, sniveling monster into a docile gentleman.

"For me?" he asked.

Sharla nodded and handed him the bouquets.

A tear fell from his eye as he grumbled, "Thank you."

From docile gentleman to ravenous fiend, Cane slobbered all over the candy canes as he gobbled them up.

"Don't eat them all at once!" Sharla warned.

"No?"

"You need to make them last a little while. Pace yourself."

"Why?"

"Because that's all you get until the candy cane field is fixed. You need to learn self-control."

Cane licked the candy canes more slowly.

"That's better," Sharla encouraged. "And don't enter Sugarplum Forest covered in humbug salt again. That's what killed all the candy canes."

"Oh," he said between long licks. Though his focus was on the candy canes, his eyes showed remorse. "Am I bad?" he finally asked.

"No, but you can never go back to Christmas Village—the humbugs will kill you next time."

"So, I *am* bad."

"No, you just need to learn to control your impulses and anger. You are too big to act recklessly. You ruin everything in your path."

"I can try."

"That's all anyone expects of you," Sharla said with a smile.

From that day forward, Cane, the peppermint yule gobbler, did a much better job controlling his sugar cravings and learned not to seek his sugar fix in Christmas Village. The clinkerbells repaired the candy cane field, and Cane was much more careful while visiting to eat his favorite candy.

Sharla returned the magic snow globe to Santa and visited Cane often. She wasn't sure what more she could do for Cane, but having a friend seemed to help him a lot. Over time, other naughties joined her and formed their own friendship with Cane and the other yule gobblers living in Merrygloom Forest.

As Cane's reputation was slowly repaired, so were the naughties'. Though they still liked mischief and shenanigans, their kindness toward the outcast creatures shined brighter than their naughtiness.

It was a grand lesson for all the creatures of Christmas: assumptions often lived far from the truth.

Cane wasn't a braindead monster filled with aimless rage—he was a sad, misunderstood giant who just wanted some candy canes.

Patience, kindness, and empathy helped Sharla and her crew shed new light on the feared yule gobblers.

Sometimes, a little bit of naughty could do a whole lot of good.

This was how the naughties saved Christmas.

Thank you for reading *The Naughty-List Elves Save Christmas*—I hope you enjoyed the story! If you have a moment, please consider leaving a review on Amazon. All feedback is very helpful and greatly appreciated!

Amazon Author Account:

www.amazon.com/author/nicolineevans

Instagram:

@nicolinenovels

Facebook:

www.facebook.com/nicolinenovels

YouTube:

@nicolinenovels

More books to come in
The Saving Christmas Chronicles!

To learn more about my other novels, please visit my official author website:

www.nicolineevans.com

Made in the USA
Columbia, SC
20 November 2024

46764159R00067